THE GIANT WITH A BIG TOE

BY
J. T. WILLIAMS

"SET YOUR IMAGINATION FREE...THEN WRITE IT DOWN"

DEDICATION

This book is dedicated to my father
For bringing the character to life
when I was a young boy
and
To my wife for her constant
encouragement
Love you always

Once upon a time
There was a giant with a big toe
He lived deep in the forest
He had no where else to go
He was a sad giant
Had no family no friends
Just a few goats and a couple of hens

He knew of the village
With buildings and shops
Full of happy
Children, moms and pops
A river and a dam
That made swimming a treat
Looks like the nicest people
You will ever meet

He longed to go there
But he dare not
He was not a foolish giant
In fact he was smart
He knew the village would rise up
In fear
When they knew the giant with the big toe
Was near

There was a young boy
In the village named
Tommy
He was a curious lad
Always Looking for adventure
And getting stern warnings
From his mom and dad
One day he entered into
The forest
As a new place to go
Not knowing of
The giant who lived there
With a big toe

The giant spent his days caring
For his animals and crops
His big toe digs the holes
The work never stops
He likes to build a fire
And cook his
Fresh caught fish
He sits and eats with always
The same wish
that he may someday
go to the village
And make some friends
But for now all he can do is pretend
He walks through the forest
Carving new paths
With his big toe
He likes to see
How far he can go

Tommy was off on a new venture
And into the forest he did go
Not knowing of the giant with the big toe
He started out early
To get the most of his day
He was not quite ready for
His encounter
You may say
Along the path he noted broken branches
and prints that looked like large feet
He knew it was impossible
But for miles the prints
Would repeat

Tommy came to a clearing
in the woods
He sat down in a beautiful field
His fatigue started to yield
He took a bite of his food
And reclined for a nap
when suddenly the ground shook
And woke Tommy with a snap
As he rubbed his eyes the
sun was bright
Then the sun disappeared
As if it were night
He sensed a strange odor
As if something was near
The sun came back
And Tommy shook with fear

What was standing in front of him
Was a giant of a man
Big head, big hands
And a huge big toe
He scrambled to his feet
But there was no where to go
As frightened as he was
He asked without detail
Was it you and your big toe
That made this great trail
The giant just stared at Tommy
In disbelief
He does not seem afraid of me
He thought in relief

My name is Tommy
I come from the village
At the beginning of the forest
I often come here to see what I can see
In all that time
I never saw you
Did you ever see me
The giant still has not said a word
And stares at Tommy who looks small
Not knowing what to say
His heart was
Skipping a beat

Finally the giant says
I live in the forest over the hill
I have always lived there
And I always will
I have seen your village
And know i cannot go
There is no room there
For a giant with a big toe

Tommy sensed that the giant
Would do him no harm
There was no reason to be frightened
Or even alarmed
The Giant appeared to be a
Sad giant who was quite shy
Tommy thought about it and wondered why
Tommy asked where is your home
Do you live with a family
Or are you alone The giant said
I live deep in the forest
With a few goats and a few hens
have no family
have no friends

Tommy said
Come with me to the village and to my home
Meet my family and friends
You don't have to be alone
The giant said
I am afraid I will frighten them all
After all I am so very tall
And what's even more concerning
You know
They have never met a giant with a big toe
Tommy thought and said
Although you may look different
You are just like me
I think all the village people will
Be able to see
So come home with me and meet the brood
We will all sit by the fire
And share some food

The giant really wanted to go
He was concerned of his looks
His height
Especially his big toe
He finally said to Tommy
I would like to go
Living in the forest is lonesome
And not easy you know
Maybe they will like me
And I can make some friends
Instead of roaming the forest
With hopes and pretense
I am willing to go and give it a try
I thank you Tommy
Your a specially nice guy
At that moment Tommy and the giant
Realized that they became friends
The giant no longer had to wish
He no longer had to pretend
So off to the village they go
Tommy perched on the shoulders
Of the giant with the big toe

As they approached the village
With each step the ground shook
The people came out of their houses and shops
For a curious look
What they saw
Was a giant with a big toe
And the young boy Tommy
Whom they all know
The people were frightened and began to shout
They were running here and there
They were running about
The giant has Tommy and we can't let that be
We must save him from the giant
You all must come with me
The people of the village gathered
With rocks, sticks, pitchforks and a hoe
The giant and Tommy had no where to go

The giant was frightened
And did not know what to say
He was afraid that the people would Treat
him that way
He knew he was different
You could tell at a glance
But those frightened and angry people
Would not give him a chance
Tommy began to shout it's okay
It was his idea to bring
The giant to town that very day
The crowd could not hear what
Tommy had to say
He was frightened that they were angry
And the giant they would slay

As the angry crowd came closer to Tommy
And the giant
You could hear what sounded like thunder
Then you heard a loud crack
Everyone turned to have a look back what
they all saw was a hole in the dam
With water rushing through it
It was bigger than a man
The crowd began to scream as the water
rushed by
If they could not fix the hole
They would all surely die
The giant looked over at the dam Then took
Tommy and gently put him on the ground
And to the dam the giant
Quickly abound

The giant did not run to the forest
Where he knew it would be safe to go
Instead he ran to the dam
And plugged the hole with his big toe
The people in the village were all in
shock
When they saw what the giant did to
save the town
The men gathered brick and mortar
And fixed the hole all around
they all now knew the giant
Was not there to hurt them
He was just different and kind
They all had different notions
They had made up their minds
Now the giant with the big toe
Was a hero
He saved the town
And a party they would throw

Its been some time since that happened
I am happy to say
Tommy and the giant are friends
To this very day
The giant still lives in the forest
With a few goats and a few hens
However back in the village he now
Has many friends

Remember all people are different
They come in all shapes and size
You should always give them a chance
And you will surely be wise
Because you never know
When you will encounter
A giant
With a
Big toe